FLAT STANLEY's
WORLDWIDE ADVENTURES 9

The US Capital
Commotion

CATCH ALL OF FLAT STANLEY'S WORLDWIDE ADVENTURES:

The Mount Rushmore Calamity

The Great Egyptian Grave Robbery

The Japanese Ninja Surprise

The Intrepid Canadian Expedition

The Amazing Mexican Secret

The African Safari Discovery

The Flying Chinese Wonders

The Australian Boomerang Bonanza

The US Capital Commotion

AND DON'T MISS ANY OF THESE OUTRAGEOUS STORIES:

Flat Stanley: His Original Adventure!

Stanley and the Magic Lamp

Invisible Stanley

Stanley's Christmas Adventure

Stanley in Space

Stanley, Flat Again!

FLAT STANLEY's WORLDWIDE ADVENTURES

BOOK No. 9

The US Capital Commotion

CREATED BY **Jeff Brown**
WRITTEN BY **Josh Greenhut**
PICTURES BY **Macky Pamintuan**

HARPER
An Imprint of HarperCollinsPublishers

Library of Congress Cataloging-in-Publication Data
Greenhut, Josh.
  The US capital commotion / created by Jeff Brown ; written by Josh Greenhut ;
pictures by Macky Pamintuan. — 1st ed.
    p. cm. — (Flat Stanley's worldwide adventures ; #9)
  ISBN 978-0-06-157436-8 (trade bdg.) — ISBN 978-0-06-143019-0 (pbk.)
  [1. Heroes—Fiction. 2. Washington (D.C.)—Fiction.] I. Brown, Jeff, 1926-2003.
II. Pamintuan, Macky, ill. III. Title. IV. Title: U.S. capital commotion.
PZ7.G84568Us 2012   2011022927
[Fic]—dc23   CIP
                                                                          AC

Typography by Alison Klapthor
12   13   14   15   16   LP/BR   10 9 8 7 6 5 4
❖
First Edition

CONTENTS

Stars and Stripes

Every Fourth of July, Stanley Lambchop dreamed of being in the local Independence Day parade—that is, until the year that his bulletin board fell on him in the middle of the night and flattened him.

"Can't I be Abraham Lincoln?" Stanley pleaded. Moments before the parade was about to begin, he found

himself sitting in the center of the Grammar Society float, with his legs folded tightly to his chest.

"I cannot tell a lie," intoned his father, George Lambchop. He towered over Stanley majestically in a white wig and ponytail. "I think you look patriotic."

"Oh, George," blushed Stanley's mother, Harriet Lambchop, who was wearing an old-fashioned blue gown and a ribbon in her hair. "You are such a good father . . . of our country. George Washington!"

Stanley's father winked. "No, Betsy Ross. It is you who deserves our gratitude for giving birth to such a fine flag." He gestured grandly down toward

Stanley, and Mrs. Lambchop curtsied with a giggle.

"How many times do I have to tell you," interrupted Stanley, "I don't want to be the—"

His younger brother, Arthur, appeared from the other side of the float. Arthur had stretched a pale bathing cap over his head and had fringed it with strands from an old gray mop. "It's not too late to be my kite, Stanley!" He peered down at Stanley from over his tiny spectacles and patted his huge belly, which was actually a pillow stuffed under his shirt.

"I beg your pardon, Mr. Benjamin

Franklin," their father said, shaking his head gravely. "I cannot allow your brother to be struck by lightning."

"Aw," said Arthur. "Even if it means discovering electricity?"

Suddenly, a nearby brass band launched into a bouncy rendition of "America the Beautiful." The float lurched forward.

"The parade is starting!" squealed Stanley's mother. She picked up a wooden pole and poked it at Stanley. "Stanley, get up! You have to wave!"

"Can't I just wave with my hands," Stanley said, "like everyone else?"

"No!" his family shouted.

Stanley let out a sigh, grabbed on to

the top of the pole, and slowly unfurled his body.

His mother had spent days sewing his costume. Thirteen red and white stripes ran down to his toes, while a square of blue with white stars covered half of his chest. He began swishing back and forth, as if he were fluttering in the breeze.

"Check out the Stars and Stripes!" someone yelled.

"Hey, flag boy!" someone called. "Smile!"

A local television crew ran up and hopped alongside the float. Everywhere Stanley looked, people were pointing their fingers at him.

Being flat had given Stanley the opportunity to do things most people never dreamed of. He had traveled around the world by airmail. He could slide under doors, slip between bars, and fold himself into an origami ninja throwing star. He had served as a cape used by the great matador Carmen del Junco in Mexico and performed with the acrobatic twins known as the Flying Chinese Wonders in Beijing.

But being flat didn't always make Stanley feel good. Sometimes, he felt as if people paid attention to him not because of who he was, but merely because of how he looked.

The only reason everyone is so excited, thought Stanley as the float rolled on, is that I look weird.

Around him, his father, mother, and brother waved excitedly to the screaming throng of people. Meanwhile, Stanley's body kept on waving, but he didn't even feel like he was there.

* * *

The next morning, Stanley was examining himself in the mirror that hung on the back of his bedroom door. He turned to the side, and it was as if his body suddenly disappeared. After all, he was only half an inch thick.

Suddenly, the door flew open.

"Guess who's on the front page of the newspaper!" shouted Arthur.

"Thanks for knocking," Stanley grumbled. He pushed the door, and it swung away from the wall where he'd been abruptly flattened once again.

"It's my room, too," huffed Arthur. "Anyway, look!"

Sure enough, there was a photograph of the Lambchops atop the parade float—and right in the middle was Stanley, swinging from his mother's flagpole. WHAT A COUNTRY! blared the headline.

Just then, the telephone rang. "George," called Stanley's mother a moment later. "It's a journalist from WUSA. They're asking about our very own flag—Stanley!"

Stanley felt something rise up from deep inside him. "I AM NOT A FLAG!" he screamed.

Arthur gaped at Stanley, and suddenly, both their parents were standing in the doorway.

"Stanley," his mother said slowly. "Are you feeling all right?"

Without answering, Stanley sprinted straight to the living room and slid under the couch, where nobody could bother him.

The Governor's Visit

The fabric on the couch's bottom bobbed up and down just above Stanley's nose. Arthur was bouncing on it, flipping channels on TV. "We're on this channel, too!" Arthur cried happily.

Stanley shut his eyes and sighed heavily.

I wish I'd never been flattened, he thought.

The phone had been ringing all morning. Every time, it was another journalist asking to speak with Stanley, who wouldn't come out from under the couch.

Then the doorbell rang. From his hiding place, Stanley called, "I'm not here!"

"He's just overwhelmed, George," he heard his mother murmur.

The doorbell rang again. Stanley heard his father clear his throat, open the door, and say, "I'm sorry, but—"

Stanley's parents gasped.

"You're not a reporter," sputtered Mr. Lambchop. "You're—you're—"

"The governor!" a voice boomed.

"And this here is Officer Williams and Officer Parker!"

"Wow," Arthur's voice whispered. "Cops."

"We're here for Mr. Stanley Lambchop!" the governor announced.

"You're here for—" began Stanley's mother tentatively.

Stanley's heart raced. It was the governor! Of the whole state!

"Well?" boomed the governor. "Where is he?"

Nobody spoke.

Stanley knew that his family was thinking the same thing he was: Sliding out from beneath a couch is no way to introduce yourself to a very important person.

"I was afraid of this," murmured the governor. "Mr. and Mrs. Lambchop, may we come in?"

Stanley saw a pair of cowboy boots and two pairs of very well-shined shoes.

"Can you tell us the last time you saw your son, ma'am?" said the black shoes.

"Why, just this morning," replied Stanley's mother's toe, which was tapping nervously.

"And where was that?" the brown shoes inquired.

"In his room," answered Mrs. Lambchop.

"Great Gettysburg!" murmured the governor's boots. "They took the boy from his own room! Don't you worry," the boots declared. "You can rest assured we will have the United States government on the case. Those kidnappers will be sorry they ever thought to mess with an American hero!"

"Kidnappers!?" cried Mr. and Mrs. Lambchop.

"American hero?" said Stanley.

The cowboy boots and the shined shoes all turned toward the couch.

"Who said that?" whispered the governor.

Stanley poked his head out from under the couch. "I did?"

"Holy Declaration of Independence!" The governor jumped in surprise.

"I was just, um . . . ," Stanley got to his feet, "cleaning up underneath the couch." He picked a piece of fluff off his shirt.

The police officers relaxed their stance, and the governor extended an enormous hand. "It's an honor to meet you, young man."

Stanley shook his hand. "My mom sewed the costume," he stammered. "It really wasn't my idea."

"Don't be bashful," said the governor. "Be proud. We need more heroes like you."

"But I didn't—"

"America can't get enough of this

young man!" The governor clapped Stanley on the back. "You're on the cover of every newspaper in the nation!"

"I was Ben Franklin!" said Arthur.

The governor mussed Arthur's hair. "Of course you were! No hero stands alone, my boy!"

Arthur frowned.

"Stanley, we're here to escort you and your family to Washington. Pack your bags. The chopper lifts off in thirty minutes."

"Washington, DC?" said Mrs. Lambchop.

"But why?" said Stanley.

"For the ceremony, of course!"

laughed the governor.

The Lambchops exchanged confused looks.

"Wait a second. Are you saying you don't know?"

The governor squared his shoulders. "Stanley Lambchop, by the order of the president of the United States of America, you are to receive the National Medal of Achievement."

Both of the police officers saluted Stanley.

"Oh, brother," said Arthur under his breath.

Mr. and Mrs. Lambchop glared at him. "Oh, brother," Arthur repeated, rolling his eyes. *I'm so proud of you.*

A Hero's Welcome

The military helicopter zoomed through the sky over America. Inside, the governor briefed the Lambchops.

"The National Medal of Achievement," the governor explained, "has been awarded to the greatest scientists, artists, and political leaders in American history."

"But I didn't *do* anything," Stanley said quietly.

"Leaping Liberty Bell! That's not what I read," said the governor. "I read that you saved Mount Rushmore!"

"He was only a Band-aid on one of the foreheads," grumbled Arthur. Stanley nodded in agreement.

The governor punched Stanley's shoulder playfully, and it bent backward for a moment like the corner of a piece of paper. "Stanley," he said admiringly, "there is nothing more heroic than humility."

Stanley turned and gazed out the window. They had passed over yellow prairies and green, rolling hills. Now, they were moments from landing in Washington, DC. He knew he was supposed to be excited, but he felt that someone had made a terrible mistake.

"You'll be under twenty-four-hour guard during your stay in the capital, Stanley," said the governor. "We can't risk an international incident."

"Do you think Stanley is in danger?" Mrs. Lambchop said, shooting an anxious look at Stanley's father.

The governor leaned forward. "Did *you* think he was in danger the night you lay him down to sleep under an innocent-looking bulletin board?"

Stanley's parents' eyes widened.

"Don't worry, we'll take good care

of him, ma'am," said one of the officers sitting behind them.

"Look!" cried Arthur.

Out the window, the top of a thin white tower loomed, looking close enough to touch.

"The Washington Monument," said the governor. "Built to honor our first president, General George Washington. Begun in 1848, and not completed until another forty years later. At the time, it was the tallest building on Earth."

As the helicopter touched down a few moments later, Stanley glimpsed an enormous crowd of people waving American flags. "Ready, Stanley?" asked the governor.

Stanley had looked into the eyes of sneak thieves while hiding in a painting at the National Museum. He had been kidnapped by spies in Mexico and foiled grave robbers in Egypt.

But he had never been more frightened than this. There was a rustling in his ears, and he realized his whole body was shaking like a leaf.

I shouldn't be here, he thought desperately.

Stanley's parents took his hands as the door swung open, and his feet were immediately blown out from beneath him by the helicopter's rotors. He flapped wildly between his mother and father.

But then the rotors slowed to a stop, and Stanley realized that the roar he was hearing wasn't the helicopter. It was the sea of people before him.

Even more shocking, they weren't waving flags. They were waving . . . Stanleys. There were hundreds and hundreds of posters cut out to look like Stanley in his flag costume.

"Flat Stanley! Flat Stanley! Flat Stanley!" The crowd surged forward. A screaming girl tried to grab Stanley's head. Someone stepped on his leg, and Stanley imagined a piece of dough being fed into a rolling machine.

I'll be trampled! he thought.

In a panic, Stanley broke free from

his parents' grip. He twisted his body and squeezed between two people and then two more, using his flatness to slide through the tight spaces in the crowd. His ears rang with people screaming his name. He slipped and

slid and squeezed on and on. Finally, the crowd started to thin out, and he bent his legs beneath him. Now he was a blur, springing through the air, hopping the way he'd learned from the kangaroos in Australia.

And before he realized what he was doing, Stanley Lambchop was running away.

We the People

Stanley spotted a pair of police officers strolling toward him. He looked around for a place to hide before he was spotted.

Then he saw it: a big framed poster, taller than he was, hung on a side of the building. It showed a crowd of smiling people of every possible shape and shade, wearing traditional garb from all over the world. At the top were the words WE THE PEOPLE.

Stanley leaped up and balanced inside the frame, plastering his face into a smile. He silently apologized to the white-bearded rabbi he was covering.

The police officers were right in front of him! Their walkie-talkies crackled.

"Calling all forces! National hero misplaced. Description: eleven years old, less than one inch thick, brown hair. Possible kidnapping."

"Let's go!" said one of the officers, and they raced away.

Stanley allowed himself a sigh of relief . . . until he noticed two men on the other side of the boulevard. They were both wearing dark suits and sunglasses, and they were staring right at him. They started crossing the street, weaving between cars, their pace quickening.

A chill went down Stanley's body.

WE THE PEOPLE

Kidnappers! he thought.

At that moment, a crowd of people came marching down the sidewalk, chanting, "Change the law! Do what's right! Truth and justice must unite!"

The two men were pushing their way through the crowd. A placard held high by a marcher, reading AND JUSTICE FOR ALL, slid before Stanley's eyes. He jumped for it.

Hanging off the back of the sign, Stanley glanced back. The two men were spinning in circles in front of the WE THE PEOPLE poster, wondering where he had gone.

I need a disguise, Stanley thought.

A block later, Stanley dived into a

recycling bin full of newspapers. He
started shoving crumpled-up handfuls
of newsprint under his shirt and into
the legs of his pants. He'd learned in
school how to fold boat-shaped hats out
of newspaper, and
now he made one and
put it on his head.

A tour group was
gathered on the giant
steps of a building
nearby. Stanley
rustled up to the
back of the group,
trying to blend in.

"Many of the most
important buildings

in Washington were burned during the War of Eighteen-twelve," the tour guide was saying. "The Library of Congress was mostly destroyed, as was the Capitol. It is said that the smoke could be seen as far away as Baltimore. Even the White House was ruined—but not before a life-size portrait of George Washington was cut out of its frame and sneaked to safety.

"We are all very lucky that the most important documents in our nation's history weren't lost during the burning of Washington. Let's go inside the National Archives and see them."

In a grand room with very high ceilings, Stanley bent over a large piece of yellow parchment, crowded with script. It was the Declaration of Independence, dated July 4, 1776. The tour guide said it was written by Thomas Jefferson. John Hancock's very fancy signature stood out among the names of all the people who had signed at the bottom.

The tour guide said that when people first came to America, many of them just wanted to be themselves without getting into trouble. They wanted the right to be different, and that was the first thing that the Declaration of Independence declared: that all people are equal and entitled to life, liberty, and the pursuit of happiness.

In the same room, Stanley saw the Constitution, which set up how the government worked: The president ran things, Congress made laws, and a Supreme Court made tough decisions. The building also had the Bill of Rights, which were the first laws to get passed and are still the most important ones. Right at the beginning, in the First Amendment, there was freedom of speech, freedom of religion, and the freedom to protest.

"Excuse me," a small voice said. Stanley turned to see two girls staring at him, holding big, colorful guidebooks. "My name is Sook-ying and this is my sister, Cho. We are from South Korea.

Are you Flat Stanley?"

"No," Stanley lied.

The girl frowned. "Your head is flat," she said. "Please, we are big fans. May I take a picture with you?"

At least it's okay to be different in America, Stanley thought. He put a crinkly, newspaper-filled arm around the girl and smiled.

Just as the camera flashed, Stanley saw two men in black suits and sunglasses appear in the doorway to the giant room: the kidnappers!

Stanley turned his back and bent his head close to the girls. "I need your help," he whispered.

A moment later, Stanley spied the

men in black as they kicked a mound of scrunched-up newspaper on the floor next to the Bill of Rights. He watched them as he escaped, sticking out of Sook-ying's backpack, folded up to look like a guidebook.

The Monumental Mistake

Stanley spent the rest of the day hiding in different museums. He visited the National Gallery of Art, where he hid from the police in three different paintings, including a Picasso. At the Smithsonian National Air and Space Museum, he was admiring the Apollo 11 space capsule, which had landed on the moon, when the men in black appeared again. Stanley gave them the slip by jumping into an astronaut suit whose visor was open. He found it to be very warm and slightly musty.

In the Smithsonian National Museum of Natural History, Stanley saw the Hope Diamond, an enormous forty-five-and-one-half-carat jewel. I wish Calamity Jasper could see this, he thought, thinking of his and Arthur's treasure-hunting friend from Mount Rushmore.

But night eventually fell.

All the museums closed.

And Stanley had nowhere to go.

He saw the Lincoln Memorial shining brightly in the dark, like a lit house on a stormy night. It sat at one end of a large strip of grass called the National Mall. At the other end, exactly one mile away, was the dome of the US Capitol, where the members of Congress worked. And right in the middle, halfway between the Lincoln Memorial and the Capitol, was the tall white pillar of the Washington Monument.

Stanley settled into Abraham Lincoln's enormous white stone lap and sighed deeply. The statue's wise eyes looked unblinkingly over him.

"I've never run away before," Stanley admitted. "Everyone must be worried sick."

Stanley smiled for a moment, thinking

of how his mother would correct his grammar. "Stanley," she would have said, "you mean that everyone is sick with worry."

"But if I go back," Stanley continued in a soft voice, "they'll make me out to be some kind of American hero. But I'm *not* one. I'm just a kid who got flattened by a falling bulletin board. Thomas Jefferson wrote the Declaration of Independence even though he knew he was going to get in big trouble with the king of England—that's a hero. Neil Armstrong walked on the moon— that's a hero. Heroes risk everything for what they believe in. They make tough choices, like you did, President

Lincoln. I didn't *choose* to be flat. I don't stand for *anything*."

Stanley looked up at Abraham Lincoln's large, impassive face. And all of a sudden, from a certain angle, the former president looked like the Japanese movie star Oda Nobu, with his big nose and square jaw and beard. Stanley's mind raced back to a moment on a Japanese bullet train, and he could hear Oda Nobu's voice in his mind.

"Stanley-san," Oda Nobu had said, "your flatness is what makes you special. But you must remember this: Being flat is *what* you are. It is not *who* you are. *Who* you are is a very bright, very funny, very curious young boy. It

is who you are, flat or round. Always remember that, Stanley-san. Flat or round."

Somehow, the memory made Stanley feel a bit better. Maybe he wasn't a hero. But at least he was himself.

Suddenly, a pair of shadows darted across the base of the statue. Before he knew it, he was surrounded by at least a dozen men in black.

"Stanley Lambchop!" one of the men shouted. "Stop—"

Stanley flipped up into the air. He sprang end over end down the grand steps, the men close behind him.

There was a long rectangular pool in front of the Lincoln Memorial. In the darkness, Stanley could see the Washington Monument reflected in and rising above it. Picking up speed, he launched himself over the water and pushed out his stomach.

Stanley skipped on the surface like a stone: one . . . two . . . three . . . four . . . five times. Out of the corner of his eye, he could see men in black racing alongside the edge of the pool, their ties flapping over their shoulders.

With a final, powerful thrust of his belly against the water's surface, he soared out of the pool . . . and landed

flat against the side of the Washington Monument.

Because he was damp from the reflecting pool, he stuck to it like a wet washcloth on the side of a bathtub.

"Stanley!" one of the men in black called. "Stop!"

"Why should I listen to a kidnapper like you?!" Stanley shouted back.

Stanley looked toward the sky and began inching his way up the monument as fast as he could. Like an inchworm, he would unpeel his arms from the stone, re-stick them a few inches higher up, unpeel the rest of his body, and pull himself up.

When Stanley finally looked down,

his stomach lurched. He was more than five hundred feet high. He reached up again, and the stone tilted. He had reached the pyramid-shaped tip of the Washington Monument.

He had no place left to run.

Suddenly, there was a blinding light and a terrible roaring. Stanley trembled as a helicopter rose into view.

"STANLEY LAMBCHOP!" a voice over a loudspeaker boomed. "STAY WHERE YOU ARE!"

The wind from the helicopter got under Stanley's skin, and his whole body flipped out to the side. He held on to the Washington Monument in desperation, his body flapping like a

flag over the capital.

"STANLEY!" the loudspeaker called. "STOP!"

In his head, Stanley heard the words of Billy Wallaby, the Australian billionaire who had brought him and Arthur to Australia. "If I were you, I'd worry about the wind, mate. That's the greatest threat to your well-being."

"Oh no," Stanley whispered.

His fingers slipped from the stone, and Stanley Lambchop flew through the sky like a shot.

The Oval Office

A half mile away, Stanley's back slammed into the dome of the Capitol with a slap. The wind was knocked out of him. For a moment, he could not even open his eyes.

When he did, there were two men in black crouched over him. Stanley sat up fast, and the side of his head smacked one of them in the nose.

"Ouch!" the man cried.

The other one held up a badge.

"Secret Service. The president wants to see you," the man panted.

"You mean you're not kidnappers?" said Stanley.

The men shook their heads.

"You're the good guys?" Stanley said blankly.

The men nodded.

Stanley flopped back down on his back. "Oops," he croaked.

Stanley waited nervously in the Oval Office. At the other end of the room was a big, empty wooden desk, surrounded by windows. A portrait of George Washington looked down at him disapprovingly.

Through a side door, a woman came in carrying a tray.

She turned to face Stanley, and he couldn't believe his eyes.

It was the president herself!

"Hi there, Stanley," she said, as if they were neighbors. "You like Mexican food, don't you?"

She put the tray down on a little table in front of a white couch, sat down, scooped some salsa onto a tortilla chip, and popped it into her mouth. She patted the seat beside her.

Stanley didn't move.

"Stanley, the president of the United

States just invited you to have a nacho with her."

Stanley quickly sat down. He carefully took a chip and placed it in his mouth.

"Nothing works up the appetite like evading the Secret Service, huh?" the president said.

Stanley swallowed. He looked at his feet awkwardly and shrugged.

"You know, it was I who decided to give you the National Medal of Achievement, Stanley," said the president. "It's quite an honor. I thought you really deserved it."

"Why?"

"Because I think you're someone we

can all look up to," she said matter-of-factly.

"You mean because I'm flat?" said Stanley glumly.

"No," replied the president. "Because you use what's different about you to make people all over the world realize what they have in common," she said. "You've traveled the globe, showing people that when they have the freedom to be different, they can achieve amazing things."

Stanley felt himself blushing. "I haven't done anything amazing."

The president raised her eyebrows. "Stanley, I'm the president of the United States of America. I've met a lot of

people who have done a lot of important things. But I don't know anyone who has saved Mount Rushmore, foiled an Egyptian antiquities thief, practiced martial arts in Japan, gone over the Canadian side of Niagara Falls without a barrel, walked across Mexico, unearthed an archaeological fraud in Africa, performed with the Flying Chinese Wonders, flown unaided across Australia—and, as of an hour ago, flapped like a flag hanging off the top of the Washington Monument while the entire world watched, glued to their televisions."

Stanley smiled. "That does sound like a lot," he admitted.

"Yes, it does," the president agreed.

Stanley munched some more tortilla chips.

"I do have one question I have been meaning to ask you," the president said. Her face became very serious. "I want you to tell me: What is La Abuela's secret ingredient?"

Stanley swallowed hard. With help from the great matador Carmen del Junco, he had traveled across Mexico to discover the famous secret ingredient in La Abuela's cooking. He had sworn he would never reveal it to anyone.

"I'm sorry," he stammered. "I can't tell you."

"Why not?"

"Because it's a secret."

The president nodded thoughtfully. "That's what a hero might say." She rose and walked toward the door that Stanley had entered from. She turned back to him. "As long as you always remember La Abuela's secret, Stanley, and hold it close to your heart, you'll be fine." She winked.

Stanley thought back to what he had learned in Mexico: *The secret is not the ingredient. It is what you do with it.*

The president looked deep into his eyes, as if to say, *That's why you're here, Stanley. Because of what you do with it.*

But how did she know?

"There are some folks who have been

very worried about you," the president said.

She swung open the doors, and Stanley saw the group of people waiting outside. For a moment, he was speechless. Then he ran up and wrapped his body around each of them, one by one.

The Award Ceremony

The following night, at the famous Kennedy Center for the Performing Arts, all of those who had traveled to Washington gathered to honor Stanley Lambchop, the youngest and flattest recipient of the National Medal of Achievement in history.

Stanley stood in a special section of seats above the audience, surrounded by his mother, father, Arthur, and the president herself. He wore a tuxedo crafted by the president's tailor, which made him feel like a special present wrapped in a very thin box. Around his neck, on a red, white, and blue–striped ribbon, hung a bronze medallion: the National Medal of Achievement.

When the orchestra finished playing the National Anthem,

everyone took their seats. The governor made some brief remarks, and then a girl in a plaid shirt, blue jeans, and a cowboy hat sauntered onto the empty stage. She carried a ukulele.

"My name is Calamity Jasper from the Black Hills of South Dakota," she said into the microphone. "I met Stanley on Mount Rushmore the day he saved Abraham Lincoln's face from cracking off. I'm real proud of him here tonight. This song is for you, cowpoke."

She gave a few strums of her ukulele and began singing in a sweet, warbling voice. The tune was "You Are My Sunshine," but she changed the lyrics to "You are our flat boy, our only flat boy." She received a standing ovation.

Mr. O. Jay Dart, the Lambchops' neighbor and the director of the National Historical Museum, appeared onstage. In great detail, he told the story of how Stanley had caught sneak thieves red-handed in his museum. An enormous screen descended at the back of the stage, and on it was projected a grainy security photograph from that night, clearly showing Stanley dressed as a shepherd girl hiding in a painting. Stanley tried to laugh even though he was embarrassed.

Amisi, the girl who had opened his envelope in Egypt and who had inspired Stanley with her intelligence and sense of justice, recited a beautiful Sufi poem.

Mountie Martin, of the Royal Canadian Mounted Police, showed an instant replay of Stanley coiled into a hockey puck, whipping past an NHL goalie to score an impossible goal.

Captain Tony, the African pilot and police officer, stood onstage with his arms around his children, Bisa and Odinga, and told of how Stanley had jumped from his plane with nothing but his body for a parachute.

The billionaire Billy Wallaby stood with his long-lost brother, Wally Wallaby, and spoke stirringly about how Stanley had reminded them of the spirit of brotherhood.

Oda Nobu, the big Japanese movie star, took the stage. "Hello, Stanley-san," he said. "You once did me the honor of traveling to Japan, because you said you were a great fan. I am here to return the favor." A great ream of paper was rolled onto the stage, and Oda Nobu tore off a gigantic sheet that was taller and wider than he was. With great speed and grace, he turned, folded, and flipped the paper this way and that—until suddenly, with a flourish, he held up an origami masterpiece shaped exactly like Stanley in real life!

A tall, dark-haired woman appeared behind Oda Nobu and held out her slender hand. "I'll take that," the great

Mexican matador Carmen del Junco said with a sly smile, whisking the intricately folded paper into the air. She swung and swooped the paper Stanley like a matador's cape in grand, dramatic arcs. It was a beautiful performance.

Yin and Yang, the Flying Chinese Wonders, thanked Stanley for teaching them the secret of balance. They transformed their bodies into a map of the United States, with a fireworks display occurring over it.

As he clapped, Stanley turned excitedly to his brother—but he wasn't there. "Where's Arthur?" he whispered.

At that moment, he was surprised to see Arthur shuffling across the stage.

"My name is Arthur Lambchop," said Arthur, as the applause died down. "I'm Stanley's little brother."

The microphone was way too tall for him, and he had to stand on his tiptoes to make himself heard. "It's not always easy having a brother like Stanley. People pay more attention to him. That's just the way it is. Plus, he gets to do stuff that my mom and dad wouldn't let me do in a million years."

Stanley saw his parents exchange worried looks.

"But," Arthur continued slowly, "I remember when we went with my dad to Africa, and Stanley got really upset because he felt alone. He was sad because there were no flat people like him. And all I could think was that nobody makes me feel less alone than my brother. He's like . . . he's like the glue that you didn't even know was there between people, bonding all of us together. When you're a kid, a lot of people ask you who your hero is. And I . . . I can't think of anybody as honest, flexible, and strong as my brother."

Stanley felt a lump in his flat throat like a golf ball.

"You're my hero, Stanley."

In the Mail

At the end of the awards ceremony, Stanley joined all the special guests onstage for the grand finale. Arthur paced before the line of performers like a general. Stanley was on the end.

"This is it!" Arthur said. "Ready?"

A murmur of excitement went down the line. Yang, the Flying Chinese Wonder, leaned forward and winked at Stanley. Stanley noticed that, beside him, Carmen del Junco and Oda Nobu were holding hands.

"Commence countdown!" Arthur hollered. "Ten, nine, eight, seven, six, five, four, three, two . . . one!"

Yin flipped high into the air and landed on her brother Yang's shoulders. Yang bent his knees, and the pair launched straight upward like a rocket. Yang landed on Oda Nobu's shoulders, so they were now three people tall. At that moment, Carmen del Junco grabbed Stanley's hands and spun him around. His feet left the ground, and she let go. Stanley arced around the theater like a boomerang, until he saw Yang's face

come into view, and they grabbed each other's hands.

Stanley held his body out to the side and waved his legs gently atop the flagpole formed by his friends.

The crowd leaped to their feet.

"That's my boy!" cried his father.

"Bravo!" yelled the president of the United States.

"Be careful!" cried Stanley's mother.

High over his friends from all over the world, Stanley waved his body proudly.

"Now me!" called Arthur.

That spring, Arthur and Stanley were playing in their room at home when their mother burst in. "Look!" she cried, waving an enormous envelope.

"What is it?" asked Stanley.

"Open it!" said his mother.

The envelope was made of thick, creamy paper, and Stanley slipped his finger under the flap and slit it open.

He pulled out a grand square of paper and read:

You are cordially invited to join us in celebrating our wedding

Oda Nobu
of Tokyo, Japan

and

Carmen del Junco
of Mexico City, Mexico

In the corner of the invitation was a note jotted in blue pen. Stanley peeked inside the envelope and spotted something else inside. He pulled out a piece of card that was shaped just like a very small version of himself.

"What's that?" said Arthur.

"RSVP via Flat Stanley," Stanley read.

"You're starting a trend," Arthur said. He sounded impressed.

Stanley smiled to himself and walked over to his bulletin board. He looked for a free spot among all of the things tacked up there. His eyes passed over a newspaper headline from when he saved Mount Rushmore, pinned next to a postcard from Calamity Jane. There was a snapshot of him and Amisi in front of Egyptian pyramids and a picture of Oda Nobu in a karate class in Japan. Underneath one corner of an Australian boomerang, there was a picture he took at the Beijing Zoo of a ferocious-looking panda bear. There was a newspaper headline from his plunge over Niagara Falls next to a flat fish head skull from Africa. He'd had a lot of adventures, and he hoped to have many more. Near the center of the board, with its red, white, and blue ribbon hanging from a pushpin, was his National Medal of Achievement.

Stanley tacked the wedding invitation

right next to the bronze medal. He read again the note jotted in the corner:

Stanley,
Thank you for bringing us together.

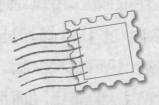

WHAT YOU NEED TO KNOW BEFORE YOUR OWN ADVENTURE IN THE CAPITAL!

Washington, DC, the District of Columbia, was named after the great discoverer Christopher Columbus.

The official flag of Washington, DC, has three red stars and two red stripes on a white background, which is based on the shield from George Washington's family coat of arms.

Although DC residents pay taxes to the federal government, they do not have a voting representative in Congress. That's why, if you drive through DC, you may see license plates that say "No Taxation without Representation!"

The National Air and Space Museum in Washington, DC, is the most popular museum in the world! More than 9 million people visit every year.

Abraham Lincoln was 6 feet, 4 inches tall, but the statue of him inside the Lincoln Memorial stands at nearly 19 feet.

The official motto of DC is Justitia Omnibus, which is Latin for "justice to all."

The White House was originally called the "Executive Mansion" or the "President's Palace." A Baltimore reporter once called it the "white house" in a newspaper article and the name caught on. Theodore Roosevelt made this the official name in 1901.

President Theodore Roosevelt kept animals in the White House for his family. They had dogs, cats, snakes, and raccoons, and a macaw named Eli Yale, and even a pony who once rode in the elevator!

The National Press Club, located in DC, is the only building in the US to have its own ZIP code!

Read the stories that started it all!

Do you know how Stanley Lambchop got to be the Flat One? Have you been following him since the very beginning? If not, here are the stories you'll want to read!

FLAT STANLEY'S
WORLDWIDE ADVENTURES 1
The Mount Rushmore Calamity

FLAT STANLEY'S
WORLDWIDE ADVENTURES 2
The Great Egyptian Grave Robbery

FLAT STANLEY'S
WORLDWIDE ADVENTURES 3
The Japanese Ninja Surprise

FLAT STANLEY'S
WORLDWIDE ADVENTURES 4
The Intrepid Canadian Expedition

FLAT STANLEY'S
WORLDWIDE ADVENTURES 5
The Amazing Mexican Secret

FLAT STANLEY'S
WORLDWIDE ADVENTURES 6
The African Safari Discovery

FLAT STANLEY'S
WORLDWIDE ADVENTURES 7
The Flying Chinese Wonders

FLAT STANLEY'S
WORLDWIDE ADVENTURES 8
The Australian Boomerang Bonanza

FLAT STANLEY'S
WORLDWIDE ADVENTURES 9
The US Capital Commotion

And we hope you'll enjoy Flat Stanley's
Worldwide Adventures!

#1 The Mount Rushmore Calamity

#2 The Great Egyptian Grave Robbery

#3 The Japanese Ninja Surprise

#4 The Intrepid Canadian Expedition

#5 The Amazing Mexican Secret

#6 The African Safari Discovery

#7 The Flying Chinese Wonders

#8 The Australian Boomerang Bonanza

#9 The US Capital Commotion

In his worldwide adventures, Flat Stanley:

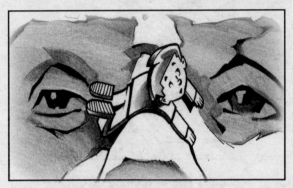

Stops Mount Rushmore from collapsing!

The whole Lambchop family is off to see Mount Rushmore. But when Flat Stanley and his brother, Arthur, team up with a scrappy cowgirl named Calamity Jasper, their vacation turns into the Wild West experience of a lifetime. Pretty soon, they find themselves in a real tight spot—even for a flat boy like Stanley.

Rescues the priceless Egyptian Giant Scrolls of Papyrus!

When you're flat like Stanley, traveling is always easy! So when Stanley receives a letter from an archaeologist, he travels by airmail to Egypt to help find an ancient treasure deep in the heart of a great pyramid. But what if even the flattest boy on earth can't wriggle out of this dark tomb—and the terrible mess he finds himself in?

Battles with deadly ninjas in Japan!

Stanley and his brother, Arthur, are such huge fans of the movie star ninja Oda Nobu that they decide to send him something even better than fan mail—Stanley himself! Soon enough, Flat Stanley is in Japan, seeing the country with his idol. But when trouble surprises them, it will take a real hero to save the day.

Floats above ski trails in Canada— as a human snowboard!

Stanley and his family are in Canada for some skiing and winter fun. But when Stanley and his friend Nick go snowboarding—with Stanley as the snowboard—they take a midair tumble . . . and find themselves floating in an amazing Canadian cross-country journey that might just be Stanley's wildest adventure yet!

Helps a famous matador in a Mexican bullfight!

When Stanley's mother needs the secret ingredient for a special recipe, Stanley mails himself to Mexico to track down its mysterious maker. But when a band of spies threatens to steal the secret, Stanley's simple trip becomes a race against an opponent that even a flat boy like himself can't slip past!

Canoes down an African river!

When a flat skull is discovered in Africa, Stanley Lambchop decides to travel there with his brother, Arthur, and their father, George. Maybe studying the skull will give them clues to Stanley's flatness. But once in

Africa, the Lambchops are in for more adventure than they bargained for. From lions to zebras to elephants, it's the safari of a lifetime!

Cartwheels over the Terracotta Army!

Ouch! Stanley accidentally caused twin acrobats Yin and Yang to take a tumble right before their Chinese New Year show. Yang's foot is broken—but luckily, Flat Stanley is flexible enough to take his place. To make up for his mistake, Stanley travels to China to help out—but can he learn all their amazing tricks in time?

And he even explores the Great Barrier Reef!
Stanley and his brother, Arthur, have

just won a trip to Australia! They fly down under on a private jet and go diving in the Great Barrier Reef. But when Arthur launches him into the air for a game of boomerang, Stanley is accidentally sent spinning into an amazing adventure deep in the heart of the Australian outback!

Flat Stanley has worldwide adventures— and you should, too!

When you're flat like Stanley Lambchop, you can pretty much travel anywhere. But that doesn't mean he's been *every*where! Whether you're going on vacation or to the grocery store, take Stanley along with you on your adventure. Snap a photo with him and log onto www.flatstanleybooks.com. Upload your photos to the Family Adventures Gallery! And while you're there, check out all the games, global facts, and more activities for kids, parents, and classrooms!